# The Cretaceous Chase

# Dinosaur Cove ™

A Cretaceous Adventure

# Dinosaur Cove™

## The Cretaceous Chase

by
REX STONE

illustrated by
MIKE SPOOR

Series created by
Working Partners Ltd

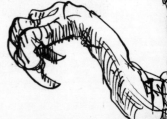

### OXFORD
UNIVERSITY PRESS

Special thanks to Jane Clarke

For Alex Dingwall, age 7, who loves Dinosaur Cove!

For Angel Browne, Kathy, Cathy, Book Week members, staff, and all the students at the Anglo American School, Sofia, Bulgaria—with thanks for making my illustration workshop visit such a wonderful experience   M.S.

# OXFORD
### UNIVERSITY PRESS

Great Clarendon Street, Oxford OX2 6DP
Oxford University Press is a department of the University of Oxford.
It furthers the University's objective of excellence in research, scholarship,
and education by publishing worldwide in

Oxford   New York

Auckland   Cape Town   Dar es Salaam   Hong Kong   Karachi
Kuala Lumpur   Madrid   Melbourne   Mexico City   Nairobi
New Delhi   Shanghai   Taipei   Toronto

With offices in

Argentina   Austria   Brazil   Chile   Czech Republic   France   Greece
Guatemala   Hungary   Italy   Japan   Poland   Portugal   Singapore
South Korea   Switzerland   Thailand   Turkey   Ukraine   Vietnam

Oxford is a registered trade mark of Oxford University Press
in the UK and in certain other countries

© Working Partners Limited 2011
Illustrations © Mike Spoor 2011

Series created by Working Partners Ltd
Dinosaur Cove is a registered trademark of Working Partners Ltd

The moral rights of the author have been asserted

Database right Oxford University Press (maker)

First published 2011
First published in this edition 2013

British Library Cataloguing in Publication Data

Data available

ISBN: 978-0-19-279392-8

1 3 5 7 9 10 8 6 4 2

Printed in Italy

Paper used in the production of this book is a natural,
recyclable product made from wood grown in sustainable forests
The manufacturing process conforms to the environmental
regulations of the country of origin

# FACT FILE

➡ JAMIE AND HIS BEST FRIEND, TOM, HAVE AN AMAZING SECRET. THEY KNOW THE WAY TO DINOSAUR WORLD! NO ONE EXCEPT THE BOYS HAS EVER BEEN THERE — UNTIL NACHO THE PUPPY FOLLOWS THEM INTO THE CRETACEOUS. AT FIRST THE BOYS THINK IT'S GREAT FUN HAVING A PUPPY WITH THEM, AND NACHO EVEN PLAYS WITH WANNA, THE BOYS' DINO FRIEND. BUT THE MOOD CHANGES WHEN NACHO DISAPPEARS. WILL THE BOYS FIND HIM BEFORE HE BUMPS INTO THE TERRIFYING ALBERTOSAURUS?

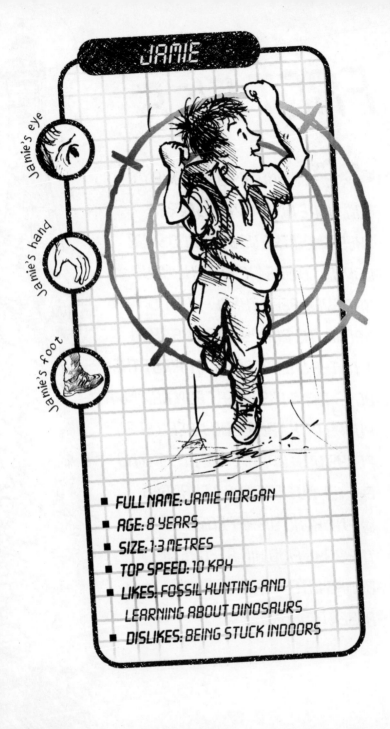

# JAMIE

Jamie's eye

Jamie's hand

Jamie's foot

- **FULL NAME: JAMIE MORGAN**
- **AGE: 8 YEARS**
- **SIZE: 1·3 METRES**
- **TOP SPEED: 10 KPH**
- **LIKES: FOSSIL HUNTING AND LEARNING ABOUT DINOSAURS**
- **DISLIKES: BEING STUCK INDOORS**

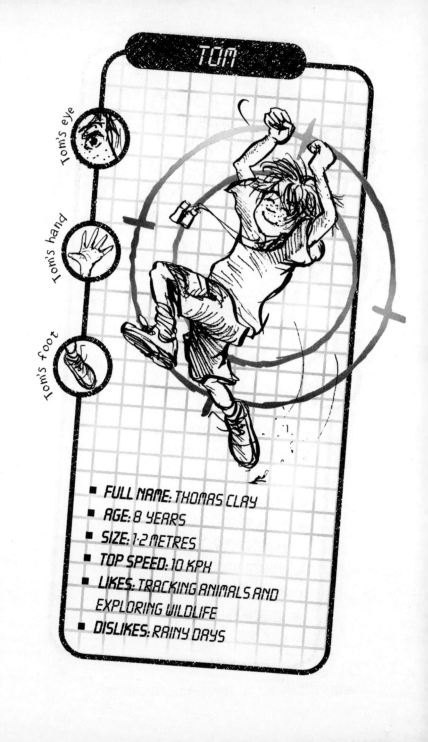

Tom's eye

Tom's hand

Tom's foot

# TOM

- **FULL NAME:** THOMAS CLAY
- **AGE:** 8 YEARS
- **SIZE:** 1·2 METRES
- **TOP SPEED:** 10 KPH
- **LIKES:** TRACKING ANIMALS AND EXPLORING WILDLIFE
- **DISLIKES:** RAINY DAYS

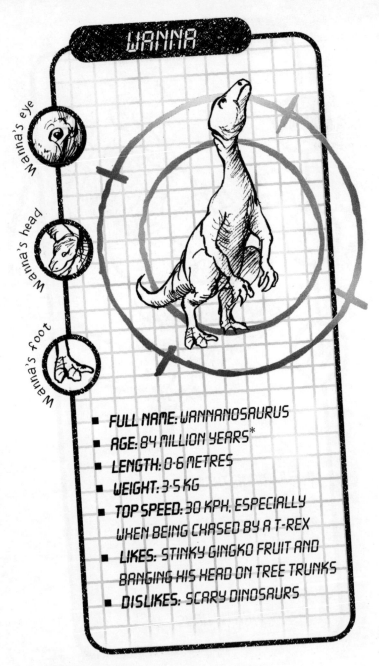

# WANNA

**Wanna's eye**

**Wanna's head**

**Wanna's foot**

- **FULL NAME:** WANNANOSAURUS
- **AGE:** 84 MILLION YEARS*
- **LENGTH:** 0·6 METRES
- **WEIGHT:** 3·5 KG
- **TOP SPEED:** 30 KPH, ESPECIALLY WHEN BEING CHASED BY A T-REX
- **LIKES:** STINKY GINGKO FRUIT AND BANGING HIS HEAD ON TREE TRUNKS
- **DISLIKES:** SCARY DINOSAURS

*NOTE: SCIENTISTS CALL THIS PERIOD THE LATE CRETACEOUS

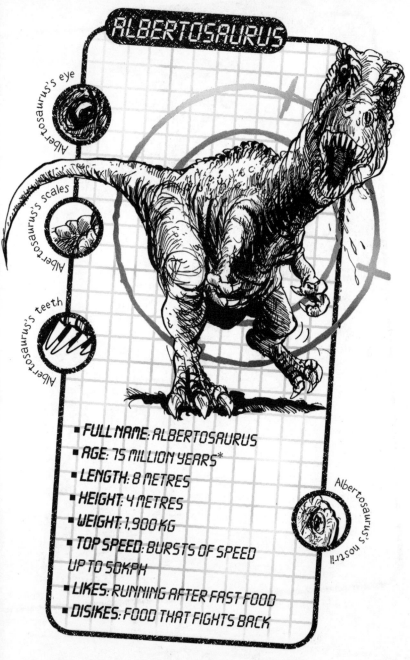

# ALBERTOSAURUS

Albertosaurus's eye

Albertosaurus's scales

Albertosaurus's teeth

Albertosaurus's nostril

- **FULL NAME:** ALBERTOSAURUS
- **AGE:** 75 MILLION YEARS*
- **LENGTH:** 8 METRES
- **HEIGHT:** 4 METRES
- **WEIGHT:** 1,900 KG
- **TOP SPEED:** BURSTS OF SPEED UP TO 50KPH
- **LIKES:** RUNNING AFTER FAST FOOD
- **DISIKES:** FOOD THAT FIGHTS BACK

**\*NOTE:** SCIENTISTS CALL THIS PERIOD THE LATE CRETACEOUS

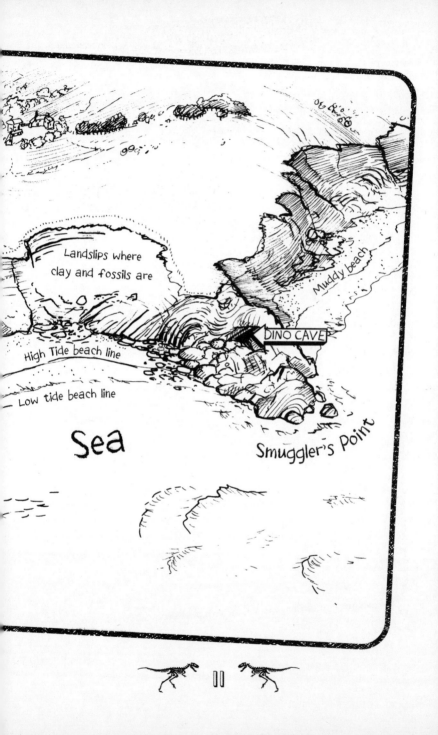

Landslips where clay and fossils are

Muddy beach

DINO CAVE

High Tide beach line

Low tide beach line

Sea

Smuggler's Point

'Nacho, fetch!' Jamie Morgan yelled,
pitching a tennis ball along the sandy
beach of Dinosaur Cove.

The shaggy Old English sheepdog
puppy yapped joyfully as he raced
after it.

'Nacho's faster than a speeding dino!' Tom Clay declared.

Tom and Jamie grinned at each other. The two friends knew just how speedy dinosaurs could be— because they'd been chased by real live ones! They'd discovered a secret cave in Dinosaur Cove that led to an amazing world full of awesome prehistoric creatures. That afternoon, they'd been about to go back to the Cretaceous for another adventure when Grandad's friend Agnes had asked them to puppy-sit.

Nacho skidded to a halt in a shower of sand. He pounced on the ball and sneezed.

*N . . . n . . . nach-oh!*

'Maybe that's why Agnes called him Nacho,' Jamie joked as the puppy

picked up the ball and hurtled back to them. He dropped the slobbery, sandy ball at Jamie's feet and gazed at him with his head cocked to one side.

'Sit!' Jamie ordered. Nacho sat. He was panting like a steam train and so were the boys.

'Let's take a breather,' Tom said. The boys plonked themselves on a ledge next to a rock-pool.

'Lie down!' Jamie told Nacho. The puppy curled up beside them.

'He's very well trained,' Tom said. 'Maybe we could do some dino training with Wanna!'

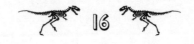

'Awesome idea!' Jamie smiled, thinking of the dinosaur friend who always joined them on their adventures. 'We'll try teaching Wanna some tricks when we get to the Cretaceous.'

Jamie took his notebook out of his backpack and opened it at the page where they'd drawn their map of Cretaceous Dino World.

'Where shall we explore this time?' Tom asked excitedly. 'Fang Rock or Misty Lagoon?'

Out of the corner of his eye, Jamie spotted a sudden movement at the base of the cliffs. Nacho's ears

pricked up and he sprang to his feet—landing in the rock-pool.

# Splash!

He bounded through it, sploshing water all over the boys, and took off towards the cliffs.

'Nacho's chasing a rabbit!' Jamie exclaimed, stowing the notebook in his backpack and jumping up.

The boys set off after him. 'Nacho!' Tom shouted at the top of his lungs. 'Come back!'

But the puppy carried on speeding after the rabbit as it zigzagged up the steep cliffside. The boys watched the rabbit bolt down its hole.

*Woof!*

Nacho barked, sticking his nose down the hole and wagging his tail excitedly.

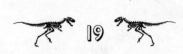

*Woof, woof, woof!*

'Here, Nacho!' Tom commanded.

Nacho started scrabbling at the rabbit hole.

'I'll try to lure him back with one of Agnes's treats,' Jamie said.

He rummaged through his backpack, pushing aside his notebook, a Cretaceous ammonite, a couple of empty doggy poo bags, a torch, and the Fossil Finder.

*Woof, woof, woof!* His fingers closed over a doggy chew and he pulled it out, tearing open the plastic wrapper.

'Yurgh!' Jamie gagged. 'It smells like baby sick! Come and get your yummy snack, Nacho!' He waved the pongy treat in the puppy's direction.

Nacho turned and sniffed the air. Then he raced down to Jamie and sat at his feet, his tongue hanging out and drool dripping from his jaws. Jamie handed him the chew. Nacho gobbled his snack and licked his slobbery lips.

'He's like Wanna with his stinky gingko fruit,' Tom declared. 'I can't wait to see him again' he added.

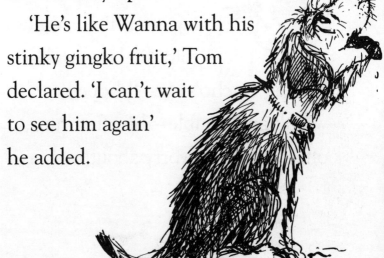

'Not long now.' Jamie pointed to a woman coming along the beach, wearing a floppy hat. 'Here comes Agnes.'

Nacho yapped in delight and ran up to his owner, wagging his tail.

'Thanks for looking after him,' Agnes told the boys as she stroked Nacho's ears. 'I hope he wasn't any trouble—he often runs off. But I don't worry about him, as he always finds his way home again. You're a clever boy, aren't you?' She patted the puppy's furry back. 'His training's coming along nicely.'

'He does sit and fetch and roll over really well,' Tom agreed.

'And he walks to heel,' Agnes said proudly, adjusting her hat. 'Now I just need to teach him to stop chasing things like cats and squirrels . . .'

'And rabbits,' Jamie added with a smile.

Agnes looked at her watch. 'Time we were getting back,' she said. 'Nacho likes his afternoon nap. Enjoy the rest of the day.'

'Will do!' Tom assured her. He glanced meaningfully at Jamie.

'Dino World here we come!' Jamie whispered.

The boys waved goodbye to Agnes and Nacho, then turned and raced up the steep cliff path and boulders to Smugglers'

Cave. They squeezed through the narrow gap at the back, into the secret cave beyond. Jamie flicked on his torch and swept the beam of light over the fossilized dino footprints that led across the floor of the cave towards what looked like a solid wall of rock. Any minute now, they'd be passing straight through it!

He felt a surge of anticipation as he fitted his foot into the first of the three-toed prints, but before he could take the next step, a scritch-scratching noise of claws on stone came from behind them.

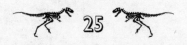

Jamie dropped his torch in surprise.

'There's something in the cave!' he whispered as the light went out.

In the pitch dark, Jamie and Tom
listened to the snuffling and scrabbling
noises coming from the other side of
the gap they had crawled through.

'What if something's escaped from
Dino World?' Tom whispered.

'It can't be from Dino World,'

Jamie hissed as noisy sniffs echoed round the secret cave. 'It would have turned to dust, like that gingko we tried to bring back.' He stepped out of the fossil footprints, groped around for his torch, and switched it on, shining it on the gap.

'It could be a badger or a fox, then,' Tom said in a low voice. 'They can be

fierce
if they're
cornered.

I hope it doesn't find us . . .'

*Sniff!*

The sound was louder. The creature growled and scrabbled some more at the stone.

'Sounds like a wolf that's got out of the wildlife park,' Jamie whispered nervously.

*SNIFF!*

A hairy snout poked through the gap.

'It's coming for us!' Tom gasped, hurriedly stepping into the stone footprints. 'Quick! Let's get into Dino World and leave it behind.'

There was a flash of light as Tom disappeared. Jamie followed close behind. As he

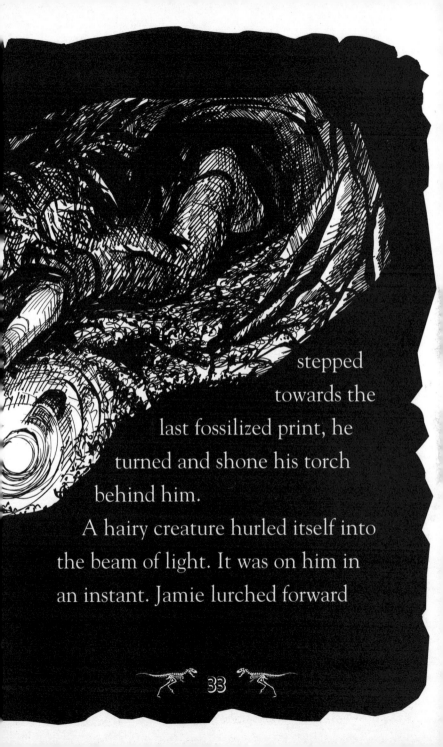

stepped
towards the
last fossilized print, he
turned and shone his torch
behind him.

A hairy creature hurled itself into
the beam of light. It was on him in
an instant. Jamie lurched forward

under the creature's weight, and his foot landed heavily in the final footprint.

There was another tremendous flash, and Jamie fell onto the warm spongy ground inside Gingko Cave, with the creature on top of him.

*Yip, yip, yip!*

It barked excitedly, licking his face with its wet pink tongue.

'Nacho!' Tom laughed. 'Jamie thought you were a wolf. That makes him a wombat!'

'Nacho's great-great-great-great-great-great-grandfather *might* have been a wolf,' Jamie said indignantly, pushing the fluffy puppy off his chest.

'You'd need a lot more greats than that,' Tom said. 'A wolf would have to evolve *a lot* to turn into Nacho!'

Jamie jumped to his feet, brushing off dead pine needles, bits of fern, and gingko leaves. He breathed in the warm moist air and the compost-like smell of the Cretaceous jungle. The air hummed with the noise of a zillion buzzing insects. It was fantastic to be back in the Cretaceous.

Nacho's tail wagged excitedly as he stuck his nose into the layer of leaf mould that covered the ground and snuffled deeply.

*N-nach-ho!*

He sneezed.

'Cool!' Jamie said. 'He's the first ever dog in Dino World!'

'We're going to have to keep a close eye on him,' Tom murmured.

*Woof!* Nacho's tail stopped wagging and stuck straight into the air. He put his nose to the ground and bounded off into the ferns that grew between the gingko trees.

'He's picked up a scent,' Jamie groaned.

'Nacho! Come back!' the boys yelled as they hurtled after him.

The puppy scampered back and forth between the gingko trees, his nose skimming over the sludgy fruits that had splattered down from the trees.

'What's he tracking?' Tom panted.

'Dunno. All I can smell is gingko stink.' Jamie skidded on a pool of gingko slime that looked and smelt like rotten carrot sludge.

Ahead of them, Nacho had stopped at a fern-covered clearing in the trees.

*Woof woof woof!*

A bony head poked out of the ferns, followed by an upright lizard-like body.

The dinosaur wagged its scaly tail.

*Grunk?*

'Wanna!' Jamie and Tom exclaimed.

Their dinosaur friend glanced nervously at the barking puppy. Then he trotted out of the ferns towards Jamie and Tom. But before he could reach them, Nacho bounded up to the little wannanosaurus.

Wanna froze. His tail drooped as the sheepdog puppy ran circles around him.

*Grunk?*

'He's never seen a dog before,' Jamie commented. 'He doesn't know what to make of him.'

Nacho crouched down in front of Wanna, his tail thumping the ground.

*Yip, yip, yip.*

'Nacho wants to play,' Tom chuckled.

'I don't think Wanna does,' Jamie said.

Nacho sprang up on his back legs and tried to pounce on Wanna. The

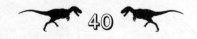

dinosaur grunked in alarm and
lowered his bony skull in self-
defence. Nacho ran into it.

### Aooo!

Nacho howled, bouncing off
Wanna's hard head. He ran behind
Tom's legs.

*Grunk,*

> *grunk,*

>> *grunk!*

Wanna skittered across to Jamie
and hid behind him.

Jamie and Tom looked at each other.

'What a pair of wombats,' Jamie chuckled. 'Now we have to help a dog and a dino make friends.'

Jamie twisted round and patted Wanna on his scaly nose.

'It's OK, Wanna,' he murmured. 'Nacho's a friend.'

Wanna's tail twitched and he stuck his head out from behind the shelter of Jamie's body.

Tom squatted down and
stroked Nacho's ears. Then
he took hold of Nacho's
collar and slowly
coaxed him
towards Jamie
and Wanna.
Nacho
stretched
his                                          nose
                                          towards
                                      the little
                                  dinosaur.
                              Jamie held his
                          breath as the two
                      creatures slowly

moved towards each other. Finally,
Wanna bumped his cool scaly dino
muzzle against Nacho's warm
rubbery nose, surrounded by its halo
of fluffy hair. Their tails began to
wag.

'That's it—make friends!' Jamie
said.

Wanna trotted in a circle around
the puppy. Nacho began to sniff at
the dino's bottom.

*N-acho!*

Nacho sneezed.

*Grunk!*

Wanna leapt into the air in
surprise.

'Imagine if we made friends like that!' Tom snorted with laughter.

'At least it's working,' Jamie chuckled as Wanna gently nudged the sheepdog puppy. Nacho raced round the little dino, nipping playfully at his toes, making him hop from foot to foot.

'Better make this a quick visit to Dino World,' Tom told Jamie as they watched Wanna and Nacho tumble around the ferns. 'We have to get Nacho home for his nap before Agnes starts worrying.'

'We'll just stay long enough to get Nacho to help us teach Wanna some dog tricks,' Jamie agreed.

Tom grinned. 'He's already started—look!'

At the edge of the ferns, Wanna was watching Nacho roll in gingko goo.

*Grunk!*

Wanna lowered his head and rubbed his cheek into the pongy sludge,

then he pivoted on his shoulder
and landed on his back with a
glubby splat.

'Maybe this isn't the best place for
dino training,' Jamie groaned as
Wanna and Nacho gleefully kicked
their back legs up in the air,
writhing in the stinky slime.

'Let's take 'em to the Great
Plains for a bit,' Tom said.

'There's more space there.'

'Awesome idea!' Jamie
picked a handful of firm
gingko fruit from a
nearby tree.

'Here, Wanna!'
he called.

The dino leapt to his feet and dashed up to him. Jamie handed him a gingko and put the rest in his backpack.

'Gingkoes are great dino training treats,' Tom commented, as Wanna chomped noisily.

Nacho ran up, his fur matted with gingko grunge. He licked at the slobbery juice that dripped down Wanna's chin. His furry muzzle wrinkled and he spat it out.

'He only likes gingkoes on his outside, not his inside!' Tom laughed.

'Come on, you two stinkbombs; we're going to the Great Plains.' Jamie pulled out the compass from his backpack.

'That's north, across the river,' Tom reminded him.

Jamie lined up the compass arrow with north and the four of them set off, scrambling down the steep slopes of Gingko Hill, into the Cretaceous jungle. They pushed through the long emerald-green creepers that hung down from the tall conifer trees and

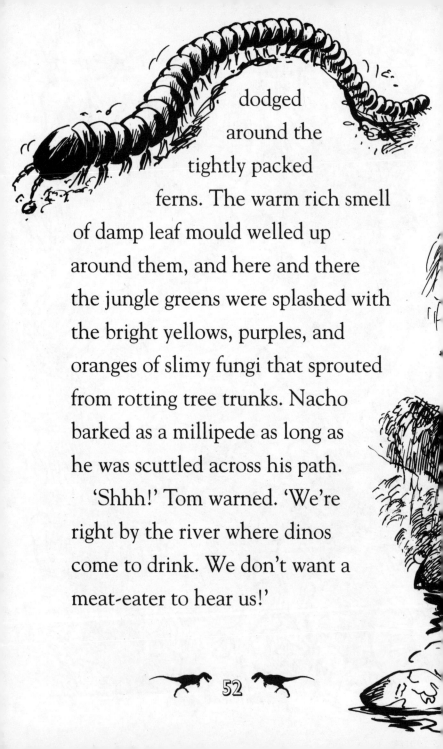

dodged
around the
tightly packed
ferns. The warm rich smell
of damp leaf mould welled up
around them, and here and there
the jungle greens were splashed with
the bright yellows, purples, and
oranges of slimy fungi that sprouted
from rotting tree trunks. Nacho
barked as a millipede as long as
he was scuttled across his path.

'Shhh!' Tom warned. 'We're
right by the river where dinos
come to drink. We don't want a
meat-eater to hear us!'

Jamie cautiously pushed through a curtain of creepers and caught his breath. Not far upriver, a duck-billed dinosaur was standing at the water's edge. It was dappled green, like the jungle.

'Coast's clear of meat-eaters,'
Jamie said, beckoning to Tom,
Wanna, and Nacho to come closer.
'But there's an awesome plant-eater.'

The dino was the size of a bus and
it had a rounded bony crest at the
back of its head. They watched as it
bent down and pulled out a bunch
of waterweed in its duck-bill-shaped
mouth. They were so close they
could hear chomping and slushing
noises as it mashed up and
swallowed the weed.

'What is it?' Tom whispered.

Jamie fished out the Fossil Finder
and switched it on. The Happy

Hunting screen popped up and he typed in '*DUCK BILL WITH CREST*'. He scrolled through the list until he found a picture of a matching dino.

'*CORY-THO-SAUR-US*,' he read.

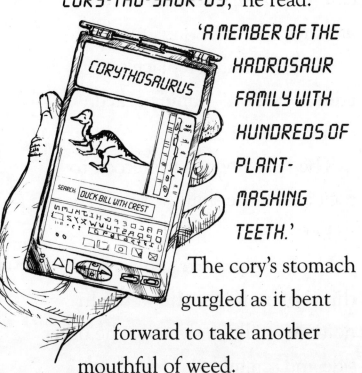

'*A MEMBER OF THE HADROSAUR FAMILY WITH HUNDREDS OF PLANT-MASHING TEETH.*'

The cory's stomach gurgled as it bent forward to take another mouthful of weed.

Wanna grunked impatiently and walked off downstream, where the river was wider and full of rocks. He stepped carefully from one rock to another.

'Wanna's found a place to cross, come on!' Jamie packed away the Fossil Finder.

The boys hopped from rock to rock across the shallow river.

*Yip!*

Nacho yelped excitedly and threw himself into the water. In no time at all, he swam to the other side and scrambled up the bank.

'Watch out, he's going to soak us!'
Tom yelled.

The ball of damp fluff shook himself from nose to tail, splattering Jamie, Tom, and Wanna with water drops.

'At least he doesn't stink so much now,' Jamie muttered as they stepped out of the green jungle into the shimmering heat of the open plains.

Tom jumped up on a boulder. He wiped the water marks off the lenses of his binoculars with his T-shirt, and put them to his eyes.

'No meat-eaters,' he said, jumping down and handing Jamie the binoculars, 'but check out the alamosaurs.'

Jamie scanned the Great Plains from right to left. Fang Rock and the Far Away Mountains were bathed in a shimmering heat haze. He twisted further to his left and surveyed the edge of the jungle.

'I see 'em!' Jamie exclaimed. 'Cool!'

He focused the binoculars on the group of heavyweight plant-eaters in the distance. As he watched, the alamosaurs turned their long necks

and sniffed the air, then went back
to grazing on the tops of the trees.

'They don't look as if anything's
worrying them. I reckon it's safe to
do some dino training,' Jamie
declared, handing the
binoculars back to Tom.

'Nacho can
demonstrate,' Tom said.
'Sit, Nacho!' He
pointed at him.

Nacho sat.

'Good dog,'
said Tom, patting him on the head.

'Sit, Wanna!' Jamie pointed at
the little dino.

Wanna turned to look behind him and his tail swept round and hit Jamie on the nose.

'Sit!' Jamie pressed down on Wanna's back.

Wanna wagged his tail and whacked him round the ear.

'I wouldn't hire you as a dino trainer,' Tom said with a giggle. 'Wanna hasn't got a clue how to sit. Let me try something else.'

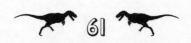

Jamie rubbed his nose and ear as Tom took a gingko out of the backpack and walked a few paces away.

'Nacho, come!' Tom shouted.

Nacho raced up to him and stood at his feet, panting eagerly. Tom ruffled his ears.

'Wanna, come!' Tom squatted on his heels and held out the gingko.

Wanna rushed towards Tom and knocked him flat on the ground in his eagerness to get at the stinky fruit.

'Great training technique,' Jamie chortled as his friend staggered to his feet.

A sudden *arooop!*
interrupted him.

It was followed quickly by calls
like a cross between a sheep's bleat
and a cow's bellow, which echoed
around the plains.

'Ankies!' Tom exclaimed in
delight as a herd of ankylosaurs

trooped out of the jungle and headed towards them.

'It's great to see them again,' Jamie agreed, remembering the time they had rescued a baby anky from a swamp and helped it get back to its herd.

Nacho crept close to Jamie's side as the huge spiky-headed herbivores rumbled past them like tanks on legs, swinging the bony clubs on the ends of their tails. Wanna watched them as he chomped up his gingko treat.

'There are a lot more babies this time,' Tom said, pointing out a

group of young ankies the size
of go-carts.

'I hope they don't attract any
predat—'

*Guuuur!*

The roar echoed
across the plains.
Jamie grabbed the
binoculars. There
was no sign of

the alamosaurs. Something else was moving between the trees. His blood ran cold as a gigantic two-legged dino with fangs like steak knives stepped out of the jungle. It gave a great snort and thundered towards them.

'Quick! Hide!' Jamie ran behind
a heap of boulders, closely followed
by Tom, Wanna, and Nacho. They
peeped through the cracks between the
rocks. The enormous killer lizard was
charging towards the herd of ankies.

'It's not a t-rex,'
Tom murmured. 'It's
more streamlined and
athletic-looking.'

'And faster,' Jamie
murmured. He
grabbed the Fossil

Finder and tapped in '*CRETACEOUS PREDATORS*'.

'*ALBERTOSAURUS*. That's it.' Jamie skimmed the page quickly. '*BURSTS OF*

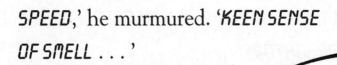

*SPEED*,' he murmured. '*KEEN SENSE OF SMELL* . . . '

He stowed the Fossil Finder and peered through a crack, just in time to see the albertosaurus charge into the herd of ankies.

*Aroop!*

They scattered

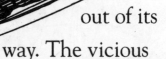

out of its way. The vicious carnivore paused for a moment, drool dripping from its fangs.

**Thwack!**

'It's hungry,' Tom murmured. Beside him, Wanna froze. Nacho's fur began to bristle.

The biggest anky took a swipe at the albie with its club. There was a *thwack!* as it connected with the predator's tail.

# Gurrrrrrr!

The albie roared with rage and lunged at the anky. The baby ankies

squeaked piteously and raced off in all directions.

The big anky turned.

*Thwack!*

Its club hit its target again, sending the predator staggering.

*Gurrrr!*

The albie slunk towards the jungle, taking backward glances at the ankies.

'It can't risk having a leg broken by the anky's club,' Tom whispered. 'It'd die of starvation if it couldn't hunt.' He trained his binoculars on the spot where the albie had disappeared into the jungle. 'I can

see ferns moving,' Tom murmured. 'It's still lurking.'

'The baby ankies have scattered all over the place,' Jamie said worriedly, pointing them out. 'They'll be easy pickings for any carnivore.'

Nacho's eyes followed his gestures. He pricked up his ears.

*Woof!*

He dashed across the plains.

'Nacho! Come back!' Jamie and Tom yelled.

*Gak-gak-gak-gak-gak.*

It sounded as if Wanna was trying to call him back, too.

 75

Nacho raced towards the
furthest baby anky and darted at the
dino's ankles. It skittered away from
him, towards the anky herd, which
was slowly moving back together.

'He's rounding the ankies up, like

they're sheep!' Jamie exclaimed.

'Well, he is a sheepdog, fossil features,' Tom said with a grin as the puppy turned his attention to another baby anky.

*Grunk!*

Wanna bounded towards a third baby anky and gently butted it towards the rest of the herd.

Tom glanced towards the jungle. 'It's not just the baby ankies who are in danger now. The albie might attack Wanna or Nacho before they manage to herd them all.'

'You're right,' Jamie agreed. 'There's only one way we can speed things up.'

He and Tom looked at each other,
then jumped out from the boulder
and ran for the nearest baby anky.

'Shoo!' Jamie yelled,
holding his arms open wide.

'Shoo!' Tom echoed.
'Shoo! Shoo!'

The little anky took one
look at the boys and
scuttled towards the safety
of the herd.

Soon all the ankies had been rounded up.

'Yay! We've got them back together!' Jamie took the binoculars and scrambled onto a big boulder to check the jungle for signs of the albertosaurus.

He looked back across the herd of ankies just in time to see the predator's tail disappear into the jungle.

'I think the albie's given up,' he said, and breathed a sigh of relief.

'It's too scared to attack the ankies now they've regrouped,' Tom said as Nacho and Wanna bounded up, panting and wagging their tails.

'We're all safe now,' he said, and gave Jamie a high five.

'Go, dino team!' Jamie grinned. He rummaged in his backpack and found a chew for the puppy and a gingko for the dinosaur. Nacho and Wanna gobbled down their treats.

'That was exciting, but now it's time we got Nacho back to Agnes,' Tom reminded Jamie as the little dino and the puppy licked their sticky lips. 'I know she said he runs away sometimes, but we don't want her to be worried about him.'

'Definitely not.' Jamie hoisted up his backpack. The boulder wobbled

as he jumped down from it, and a
rabbit-sized dino shot out from
underneath. It had a V-shaped crest
on its head that from the side
looked like bunny ears.

'It's a baby lambeosaurus,' Jamie
muttered. 'I recognize the crest from
the Fossil Finder.'

*Yip! Yip! Yip!*

Nacho bolted after it.

'Oh no!' Tom groaned.
'He's run off after a
dino-rabbit!'

83

'Come back, Nacho!' Jamie yelled.

*Grunk!*

Wanna lifted his scaly snout into the air.

Nacho glanced back at them, but carried on running.

'Sit!' Tom tried.

Wanna sat down obediently. But Nacho was still pelting after the dino-rabbit, in the direction of Fang Rock.

'Heel!' Jamie shrieked, sprinting off after the puppy. Wanna ran along next to him.

'Wanna *can* do dog tricks.' Tom panted, racing along beside them.

The dino-rabbit was heading towards the loop in the river, with Nacho snapping at its heels. The ground beneath their feet was getting soggier and soggier.

'Watch out, it's boggy here,' Jamie groaned.

Ahead of them, the lightly built
dino-rabbit scuttled across the muddy
ground as if it was solid rock. Close
on its trail, Nacho was jumping over
stagnant boggy puddles, using clumps
of ferns like stepping stones.

Jamie and Wanna leapt into the
air like hurdlers, both aiming for the
same small clump of ferns.

*Whump!*

They bounced off each other and landed in a pool of stinky mud.

*Splat!*

The mud glooped and glubbed as they struggled to their feet.

'Having fun wallowing, you pair of prehistoric hippos?' Tom chuckled, jumping carefully from

one fern clump to another. The spiral tendrils of a new fern frond tangled round his trainers, knotting his feet together.

*Splat!*

Tom landed in the mud and came up snorting.

'Now who's a prehistoric hippo?' Jamie laughed wryly.

The boys and Wanna waded through the gloopy goo and out onto firmer ground, just in time to see Nacho chase the dino-rabbit up to a weathered rock the size of a house. Nacho ran behind the rock, barking wildly.

There was a sudden yelp and Nacho came shooting out again, his tail between his legs. He glanced back over his shoulder, shaking all over.

'*Uh-oh!*' Tom groaned as a huge dino with three fearsome-looking horns and a sharp beaked mouth emerged from behind the rock. 'He's disturbed a triceratops, and it doesn't look happy!'

Jamie caught his breath. T-tops might be a plant-eater, but it was bigger than the biggest elephant at the zoo. Nacho stood rooted to

the spot as the t-tops
tossed its head and snorted
with rage at the trembling puppy.

'It looks like a bull getting ready to charge!' Tom muttered.

The ground trembled as the t-tops stamped its feet.

'Nacho will get flattened,' Jamie whispered nervously.

Suddenly there was a loud *Gak!*

Tom and Jamie glanced at each other. Wanna was revving up.

*Gak! Gak! Gak!*

Their dino friend kicked at the ground.

The t-tops's black eyes shifted from Nacho to Wanna.

It tilted the huge frill at the back of its neck towards the little dino. Its three horns faced forwards like deadly lances.

Wanna stopped kicking his feet. He lowered his bony head and stiffened as if bracing himself for impact.

'Wanna hasn't got a chance against a t-tops,' Jamie shouted. 'We have to stop it charging into him!'

CHAPTER 6

'Distract it!' Jamie yelled, shrugging off his backpack and pulling his muddy T-shirt over his head. Tom whipped off his T-shirt, too.

The two friends stood next to each other and waved their

T-shirts at the angry triceratops,
like matadors waving their capes
at a bull.

The huge beast thundered
towards them, its horns level with
the boys' chests. In the nick of time,
Jamie and Tom leapt aside,

and the t-tops charged between them.
Its sharp horns tore the T-shirts out of
the boys' hands. They flapped over the
dino's eyes, temporarily blinding it.

'That was close!' Jamie muttered.

The three-horned dino skidded to
a halt and tossed its head, shaking
off the boys' T-shirts.

Nacho cautiously slunk up behind
the huge dinosaur and grabbed
Tom's T-shirt in his jaws. Wanna
watched with his head on one side
as the puppy returned the T-shirt to

Tom and sat down obediently next to him.

Jamie's mouth dropped open as Wanna scuttled across to fetch his T-shirt.

'Awesome retrieving, Wanna,' Jamie whispered as Wanna dropped the shirt at his feet.

Tom and Jamie gripped their T-shirts in both hands, ready for the grumpy dino to turn and charge again. But the triceratops had lost

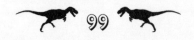

interest in them. It was staring into the distance.

Tom, Jamie, and Wanna followed its gaze. The Far Away Mountains were shrouded in a weird reddish-brown layer of fog that they hadn't noticed before.

The t-tops snorted and stomped
off across the Plains. Wanna shifted
from foot to foot, grunking
nervously.

'Maybe there's a storm brewing,'
Tom said, pulling his T-shirt over his
head. 'Let's get Nacho back home

while he's being good.'

'Before he finds anything else to chase!' Jamie agreed, putting on his shirt. It was caked with mud and dino drool and there was a tear in it from the t-tops's horn. He picked up his backpack.

As they trekked into the jungle, Nacho began to growl.

*Grrrr!*

He was quiet at first, then grew louder and louder.

Jamie looked at Tom. 'I don't think it's the storm that's bothering him . . .'

## GURRRRR!

A roar came from the trees straight ahead of them. The albie burst out, snarling ferociously.

Tom gulped as it sped towards them. 'It's been tracking us.'

'We can't outrun that!' cried Jamie. He stared in horror as the muscular long-legged carnivore quickly narrowed the gap between them.
*Woof!*

Nacho leapt to his feet and crouched in the albie's path, barking loudly. The boys watched, appalled, as the albertosaurus lunged at the puppy, gnashing its crocodile-like jaws.

*Yip!*

Nacho yelped. He flung himself onto his back, rolling over and over.

Jamie's heart skipped a beat. Was the albie going to scrunch him up?

But as the predator lunged down at
Nacho, jaws gaping wide, the puppy
jumped to his feet and ran in tight
circles around the albie's legs. The
albie twisted this way and that,
snapping its fangs at the quick-
moving puppy.

Suddenly, Nacho broke away
and dashed towards the
double prongs of
Fang Rock.

YIP!

The albertosaurus snatched at him, but missed. It lurched drunkenly from one foot to the other.

'Nacho's made it dizzy,' Tom hissed as the scaly predator tottered about. 'Let's get out of here before it gets its balance back.'

Jamie, Tom, and Wanna raced after Nacho. Jamie glanced back over his shoulder and saw the albie staggering behind them, veering from side to side. 'It's catching up!' he yelled.

They hurtled over the ferns and pushed through the few straggly creepers that hung down from the closest corner of Fang Rock. They pelted behind it, but could still hear the albie gaining ground.

Nacho huddled between the two pointy rocks, panting and exhausted. Jamie, Tom, and Wanna skidded to a halt beside him.

The albie's head appeared round
the side of the rock.
*Gurrrrrrr!*
It growled, showing its
knife-like fangs.
Jamie looked
around

wildly, but there was nowhere to hide—and if they ran, the albie would easily catch them.

Wanna hurled himself at the rockface, but it was too smooth and too steep to climb. He slid back down and huddled beside Jamie, Tom, and Nacho.

# GURRRRR!

The albertosaurus roared triumphantly.

Nacho and Wanna started to whimper.

'We're trapped,' said Jamie. A blast of the albie's breath hit him in the face, and he gagged at the stench of rotten meat.

'We're dinner!' Tom muttered.

The albertosaurus thrust its head through the V-shaped prongs of rock. It towered over them, taller than a telegraph pole. Jamie, Tom, Wanna, and Nacho held their breath as the vicious carnivore bent towards them, saliva dripping from its fangs.

A scaly
nostril brushed
across the top of
Jamie's head. The albie
was sniffing at each of them
in turn. Would it gobble them
down in one gulp, or chomp
them up bit by bit? Which one
of them would it eat first?

Jamie closed his eyes . . .

From high above his head he
heard a great roar.

'That's not the albie,' shouted Tom.

Jamie opened his eyes again and peered upwards. All he could see was the creamy-orange scales of the albie's throat. It was sniffing at the air, twisting its great jaws from side to side. Slimy strings of drool swung from its fangs.

# Gurrr!

The albie growled. Its muscular tail thwacked against the side of Fang Rock like a whip as it turned and ran away.

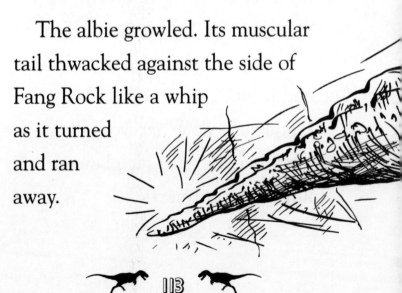

'We're alive!' Jamie and Tom leapt up and down, clapping each other on the back and patting Wanna and Nacho. Their dino and doggy friends skipped around, joyfully wagging their tails and trying to lick the boys and each other.

'Why didn't it eat us?' Jamie asked as the excitement died down.

'It could smell something,' Tom said slowly. 'Maybe something scared it off . . .'

Jamie gulped. What would scare off an albertosaurus? He glanced around nervously.

Wanna raised his scaly snout, like the albie had done, and sniffed at the air.

*Grunk, grunk, grunk!*

He stretched out his neck and tail as if he was about to run, too.

Tom and Jamie exchanged glances. Then they cautiously edged round the base of Fang Rock, rounding a clump of ferns.

*Whoosh!*

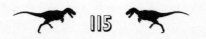

**W**hoosh!

A gust of sand-laden wind hit them in the face.

Jamie put his hands over his eyes and peered through his fingers. Ahead was what looked like a mile-high wall of reddish brown fog rolling towards them. Only it wasn't fog at all.

'It's a sandstorm!' Tom choked as the wind swirled round Fang Rock. 'And it's coming our way.'

Zillions of tiny particles lashed at them. Jamie's face felt as if it was being sandpapered.

*Grunk!*

Wanna backed into the clump of dusty ferns, closely followed by a sneezing Nacho.

'Wanna's got the right idea. Take cover!' Tom coughed, dropping to his knees and crawling into the ferns. Jamie did the same. Grains of sand were pinging off the ferns like drops of rain hitting a flat rock.

'Wanna!' Jamie yelled above the whirling wind. 'Nacho! Where are you?'

*Grunk!*

*Woof!*

The answering calls seemed to come from inside Fang Rock.

Jamie and Tom crawled out of the other side of the

dust-battered ferns. Wanna and
Nacho were huddled up together in
a shallow crevice in the base of the
rock. The boys wriggled their way in
beside them.

Outside, the ferns were being
buffeted by gale-force winds. The
hot air was filling with dust and
sand, making it hard to breathe.

'Cover your mouth and nose!'
Tom said. He pulled his T-shirt
over the lower part of his face.

Jamie shrugged off his backpack
and did the same. Behind him,
Wanna stuck his snout under the
backpack. Nacho curled up under
Tom's legs.

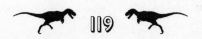

Something scuttled into the
cave.

*Woof!*

Nacho barked.

'Uh-oh,' Jamie muttered.

It was another baby

 lambeosaurus, looking
for somewhere to
shelter from the
sandstorm. But
the dino-rabbit
took one look at
Nacho, then
turned and
fled.

*Woof! Woof! Woof!*

Nacho leaped to his feet.

'You're staying here!' Tom grabbed at the puppy's collar, but he twisted out of his way and bolted after the little dinosaur.

'He's gone again,' Tom said
in despair.

'And he's picked the worst time
to run off,' added Jamie.

He scrambled to his knees and
crawled through the ferns, feeling

the whoosh of the sandy wind. He pulled his T-shirt up over his face and squinted through the hole made by the t-tops's horn. The dust and sand stung his eyes as he peered into the wind. Visibility was down to about the length of a football pitch. He could just make out Nacho running north-east, on the edge of the dust cloud, chasing the dino-rabbit towards a tall rocky pillar.

There was a surge of sandy dust and the sky darkened. It was impossible to see the difference between the earth and sky.

Nacho and the lambeosaurus were
swallowed up by the red-brown fog.

Jamie crawled back to the rocky
shelter.

'There's no way we can chase
him in this,' he yelled, raising his

voice against the shrieking wind.
'Nacho's gone!'

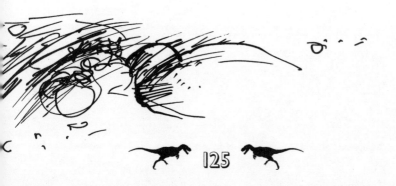

**CHAPTER 8**

The sandstorm howled round Fang Rock like a ravening beast.

Jamie, Tom, and Wanna huddled together in their rocky shelter. They looked at each other worriedly.

'All we can do is wait it out,' Tom shouted in Jamie's ear.

'You're right. But it's horrible not knowing where he is,' Jamie groaned, gazing out of the shelter.

Gusts of sand blew into the shelter, making their eyes sting. Jamie pulled his T-shirt more closely round his face, and Tom did the same.

*Splurgh-grunk!*

Wanna spat out a mouthful of sand.

'You can't breathe properly either, can you?' Tom said to the little dinosaur. He felt around in his pocket, pulled out a handkerchief and wrapped it over Wanna's mouth

and nostrils. He knotted
it at the back of
Wanna's head. The
wannanosaurus gave a
muffled *grunk* and
curled up between the two boys.
They sat in worried silence
until at last the roaring sound
faded and the sky lightened. Jamie,
Tom, and Wanna emerged from
their shelter. The boys pulled their
T-shirts away from their faces and
Wanna shook away the handkerchief. Tom stuffed it back in his
pocket. The clump of ferns had been
beaten flat and everything, including

Fang Rock, was covered with a thick gritty layer of red sand. As they walked, their feet stirred up the dust, making Wanna sneeze.

*Nach-oh!* spluttered the little dinosaur.

'Wanna sounds like he's calling for him,' Tom said. 'Good idea, Wanna!'

Both boys shouted at the top of their lungs. 'Nacho! Nacho!' But trails of sand still drifted in the air, tickling the backs of their throats. They doubled over in fits of coughing.

Wanna looked around, grunking sadly. There was no sign of the little sheepdog.

Tom knelt down to examine

the sand-strewn ground. 'No way can we track him,' he said in dismay. 'The sandstorm's blasted away his paw prints. He could be miles away by now.'

'The albie might come back and eat him,' Jamie said worriedly. A panicky feeling welled up inside him. 'How would we explain *that* to Agnes and Grandad? We have to find him!'

'Where did you last see him?' Tom asked.

'Heading that way.' Jamie pointed to the rocky pillar. 'Maybe he's still there. Come on!'

They hurried towards the pillar. Its surface was twisted and pockmarked, as if it had been blasted by countless sandstorms. Jamie's heart beat faster as they skidded to a halt beside it. In front of the pillar, the land dropped away into a hidden canyon.

It was a sunken valley with steep slopes, filled with a jumble of rocky towers, spires, and pillars. Each had horizontal

stripes made from different types of
stone, coloured in every shade of red
and gold and eroded into weird and
wonderful shapes.

'That one looks like a giant sheep,' Jamie said, pointing it out.

'And there's a skyscraper.' Tom indicated another rock.

The hundreds of rocky formations were so close together that it was hard to see a way between them.

'It's a maze,' Tom declared. 'An a-maze-ing maze!'

Jamie groaned as Tom guffawed. Wanna put his head to one side.

'Shhh!' Jamie hissed. 'Wanna can hear something.'

The boys cupped their hands to their ears and listened intently.

'*Woof!*'

The bark was faint but unmistakable. Jamie's heart leapt with joy. 'Nacho!'

He hurtled down the steep rocky slope into the canyon, Tom and Wanna beside him.

The bizarre rocks towered above them, blotting out the light and casting spooky shadows. Narrow sand-blown pathways twisted and turned between the crazy formations.

*Woof! Woof! Woof!*

Nacho's bark echoed off the canyon walls. It was impossible to pinpoint where it was coming from.

'Nacho!' Tom and Jamie yelled again.

*Cho . . . cho . . . cho . . .*

The shadowy canyon echoed back their call.

A shiver ran down Jamie's spine.

How would they ever find Nacho in here?

# CHAPTER 9

'Maybe Wanna can sniff him out,'
Tom suggested. He got down on his
hands and knees and sniffed at the
ground to show Wanna what he
meant. 'Woof!' Tom barked, wiggling
his bottom from side to side, as if he
was wagging a tail. 'Woof! Woof!'

Wanna stared at him in disbelief.

Jamie dropped to his knees and crawled after Tom, sniffing loudly.

For a moment Wanna stood looking at them as if they'd gone mad, but then their dinosaur friend dropped his snout and began to sniff too.

'That's it, Wanna,' Jamie encouraged him.

*Sniff . . . sniff . . . sniff . . .*

Wanna snuffled. Then he raced up to Jamie and nudged at his backpack.

'He doesn't get it,' Jamie groaned, standing up. 'He's sniffing out gingkoes.'

'I'll give him one.' Tom stood up as well and put his hand into the backpack. 'Yuck!' he spluttered as the ripe fruit squished between his fingers. Stinky gingko juice dripped all over the backpack and ran down Tom's arm to his elbow.

Tom held out the fruit to Wanna, who wagged his tail in delight as he

gobbled it up then
slurped the stinky slime
off Tom.

The smell of ripe
gingko lingered around them.
Jamie screwed up his face in disgust.

'Wanna might not be able to
smell Nacho, but he can definitely
smell us,' he groaned.

'That's it!' Tom said with a grin.
'We'll never be able to find Nacho
in this maze—so he can sniff us out
instead!'

'Yes!' Jamie exclaimed. 'We can
lure him to us with a smelly treat,
like we did when he was chasing

Urgh!

that rabbit
on the
beach.' He
pulled a doggy
treat out of his
backpack and
ripped open the packet.
'He can't resist these . . . '

Jamie waved the chew stick
about. Its baby-sick pong welled
around them. A sudden breeze blew
the stench back in his face.

'Urgh!' he gagged.

Tom stuck his finger in his mouth
so it was wet, then held it up. The
breeze cooled the right side of it.

'The wind's coming from that way,' he said, pointing to the right—deeper among the rocky maze. 'If we go there we'll be upwind, and the breeze can carry the dog treat scent to Nacho. Then he'll sniff us out.'

They set off into the maze. It was cooler than on the plains, and like being in a dense fairytale forest—but with rocks instead of trees. The sort of fairytale forest where witches and wolves might hang out . . .

'What's that?' Jamie jumped as a long dark shape skittered across a twisted turret of rock.

'Your shadow, you wombat,' Tom
said with a nervous laugh.

Something small and lizardy shot across the path in front of them, too fast for them to make out what it was.

Jamie half-expected to see Nacho flying after it, but instead of a bark, an unearthly *creech* echoed around them. Jamie's blood ran cold. It was unmistakably a hunting cry.

Wanna grunked and looked up, fidgeting from foot to foot.

'Is it a pterodactyl?'
Jamie murmured, gazing
into the sky.

*Creech!*

The scary sound
came again. It was
at ground level.

Tom turned to
Jamie. 'Dinosaur!'
he murmured. 'A
meat-eater lives
in this maze!'

Jamie could see
that under the

mud and freckles, his friend's face had gone pale. He gulped. 'Let's hope Nacho finds us before it does,' he said, wafting the smelly dog chew from side to side. 'And before it finds him.'

'Try not to make any noise,' Tom advised.

They tiptoed through the twisting, turning maze of strange shadowy rocks, glancing anxiously from side to side.

A patter of claws came from the far side of a rocky tower.

'Nacho!' Jamie breathed, hurrying towards the sound.

But it wasn't a dog that appeared round the rock. It was a feathered two-legged dinosaur,

as tall as a giraffe, with a snout lined with pointy fangs. The dino's shaggy blue-green feathers shimmered in the shadowy light and the sharp talons on its feet pattered against the ground as it stalked towards them.

'It's a raptor!' Tom yelled.

'Run!'

CHAPTER 10

Jamie, Tom, and Wanna raced through the maze of rocks with the giant raptor on their heels.

Jamie glanced behind to see it fan out a crest of purple feathers and lunge feet first towards them with a blood-curdling *creech!*

In the nick of time, the boys
and Wanna swung round a pillar
of rock and flattened their backs
against it. Ahead of them, the
path forked into two passageways.

The raptor shot past, and raced up the passageway on the right.

'It hasn't seen us,' Tom breathed as he, Jamie, and Wanna turned down the other path

and squeezed past a boulder the shape of a giant turtle. On one side of the path rose the steep wall of stone that formed the edge of the canyon.

*Woof!*

A loud happy bark bounced off the canyon wall. Jamie didn't know whether to laugh or cry. Nacho was nearby—but he was making so much noise that the raptor would be able to find them!

'Nacho! Shhh!' he hissed.

The sheepdog puppy emerged from the shadows and gambolled towards him, enthusiastically wagging his tail. His eyes were fixed firmly on the treat that Jamie was still clutching in his hand.

*Woof! Woof!*

He barked joyfully.

Tom peered back round the turtle-shaped rock. The raptor's glittering eyes stared back at him.

'It's found us!' he groaned. There was a sudden swishing of feathers and a clattering of claws as the raptor sprang onto the turtle-shaped rock.

Nacho looked up in amazement. He howled, dashing off with his tail between his legs. He shot into the shadows at the base of the rocky wall of the canyon, and disappeared into a hole.

 157

'Follow him!' Jamie yelled.

The giant raptor leapt into the air like a long-jumper. Jamie sprinted after Nacho, and did a rugby dive into the hole. Wanna and Tom dived in after him. When the feathered

predator tried to follow them, it clattered against the narrow opening.

'Way to go, Nacho!' Jamie cheered. He glanced around. The hole opened into a cave the size of a small car. 'We'd never have found this on our own,' he said.

The raptor's long claw came through the hole and sliced across the cave like a meat cleaver.

'Watch out!' Tom shrieked.

They leapt over the vicious claw as it swept backwards and forwards in the confined space. It was like skipping with a deadly rope. The raptor withdrew its claw.

*Creech!*

The raptor's terrible cry echoed round the tiny cave. It stuck its feathery head through the hole.

Jamie, Tom, and Wanna flattened themselves against the rock.

The raptor fixed Wanna with its sparkling green eyes. Then it turned its head to one side and opened its jaws.

Wanna
screamed.
*Gak!*

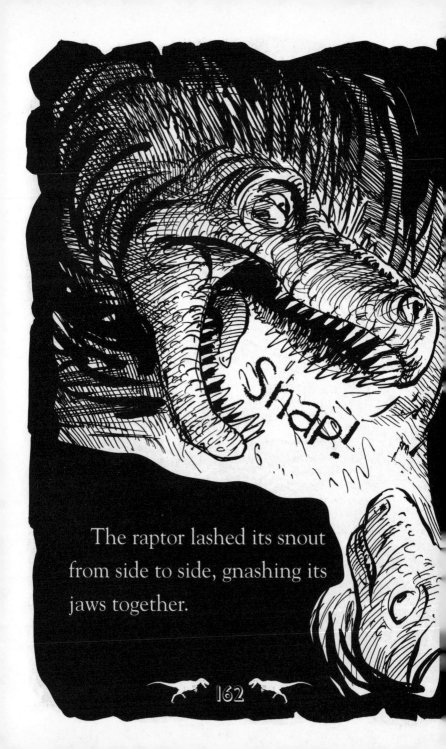

The raptor lashed its snout from side to side, gnashing its jaws together.

'It can't reach us,' Tom realized, breathing a sigh of relief.

'It's close enough!' Jamie mumbled. The stiff scaly quills of the raptor's feathery crest were brushing across his trainers, and he could see each individual scale on the raptor's snout shimmering like butterfly wings. It smelt of sweaty football boots and musty feather pillows.

With a final frustrated *creech!* the raptor's head disappeared from view. There was a pitter-pattering noise, then everything went quiet.

'We should wait for a while before we check the coast's clear,' Tom whispered.

'We've never seen a raptor *that* big before,' Jamie murmured, quietly extracting the Fossil Finder from his backpack and turning it on. He bent over the screen.

'It's a utahraptor!' he hissed, reading from the page that popped up. *THE LARGEST RAPTOR YET FOUND, ONE OF THE DEADLIEST PREDATORS EVER.*

Tom stepped away from the cave wall and cautiously peered outside. 'And it's right there, waiting for us,' he groaned. 'We can't go back that way.'

Behind them, Nacho was sniffing and scrabbling at a pile of stones.

*Woof!*

He barked softly, wagging his tail.

'He's found something,' Jamie said.

'Not another dino-rabbit,' Tom groaned. He threw himself at Nacho

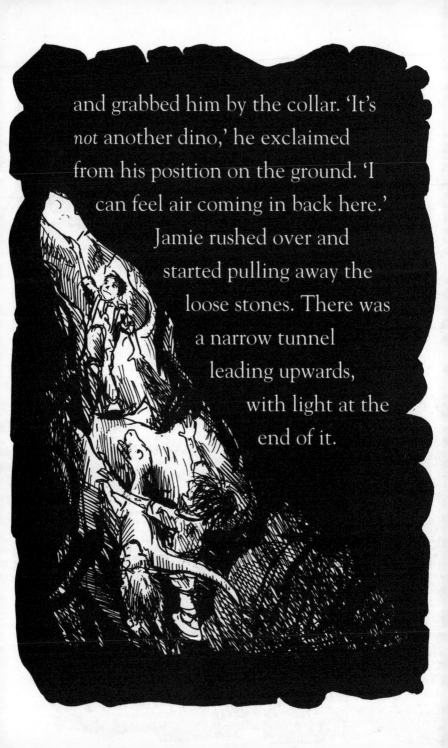

and grabbed him by the collar. 'It's *not* another dino,' he exclaimed from his position on the ground. 'I can feel air coming in back here.' Jamie rushed over and started pulling away the loose stones. There was a narrow tunnel leading upwards, with light at the end of it.

'Clever boy!' he told Nacho. 'You
found a secret escape route.'

They scrambled up the narrow
dark tunnel and pulled themselves
out, blinking in the daylight. They
had emerged onto the sandy grass,
right by Fang Rock. Wanna and
Nacho danced around them
in glee.

'Aw, they're happy we're all back together,' Tom said.

'I'm happy we're all in one piece!' said Jamie.

He gave Wanna and Nacho a dino and dog treat to celebrate. Wanna gulped down his gingko and rubbed his head lovingly against Nacho, and the little puppy rolled over and let him gently butt his tummy, leaving a trail of gingko drool.

'Let's get him back to Agnes before he causes any more trouble,' said Tom, tickling Nacho behind the ears. 'Wish we had a lead.'

'Why don't we make one?' Jamie suggested.

He tugged down a straggly creeper that was dangling from Fang Rock. He stripped off the leaves and tied it through Nacho's collar.

'Right, Nacho,' Jamie said, taking hold of the end of the lead. 'Now it really, really is time to go home. We've all had plenty of adventure for one trip!'

Tom, Jamie, and Nacho turned
to go.

*Grunk!*

Wanna sat down and refused
to budge.

'He wants a collar
and lead, too!' Tom
laughed. He tugged
down a couple more
creepers and tied
one round Wanna's
scaly neck, taking
care that it wasn't

too tight. Then he tied a creeper
lead like Nacho's to Wanna's collar.
Wanna trotted proudly beside Tom
as they headed across the Plains
towards Gingko Hill.

'What's it like, walking a pet
dino?' Jamie asked him.

'Awesome!' Tom grinned.

But as Tom spoke, their dino
friend froze and glanced wildly
around. Tom pulled on the creeper
lead, but Wanna dug in his heels.

Jamie and Nacho stopped too.

Jamie held his breath.

He could hear a rumbling noise, and it was coming closer. The ground began to shake.

'It's the albie again,' he groaned. 'And there's nowhere to hide!'

CHAPTER 11

'Freeze!' Tom cried as the predator thundered towards them, kicking up a cloud of dust. 'Movement catches its attention,' he hissed. 'It might lose interest if we don't move.'

Jamie could feel Nacho and Wanna shaking with fear.

The
albertosaurus
paused and
sniffed at the
ground.

'It's still
interested,' Tom
muttered.

Nacho pulled the
lead out of Jamie's
hand and raced
towards the albie,
barking furiously as
he ran rings round it.
But this time the albie
wasn't distracted.

Its beady eyes were fixed on Wanna,
Tom, and Jamie and it strutted
towards them, gnashing its teeth.
Nacho ran back to them and hid
behind Jamie's legs.

Jamie's blood
ran cold. There was
no hiding place and no
sandstorm to save
them now.
The albertosaurus
opened its fearsome jaws.
It was dribbling.

# Gurrr!

It roared.

Jamie wondered if it would hurt to be eaten. He squeezed his eyes shut and waited for the final chomp.

The ground beneath his feet rumbled. He didn't feel the albie's jaws closing over him —instead, there was a familiar bellow from behind.

# Aroop!

Jamie swung round.

The ankies were back! They trooped towards the albertosaurus.

176

The predator turned
and stared at
them as they
surrounded it.
Jamie
glanced at
Tom. He was
grinning from
ear to ear.
He held up an
imaginary microphone.

Aroop!

'Right in front of our eyes,' Tom said in his wildlife presenter's voice, 'we're witnessing an amazing real-life drama. A hungry albertosaurus has been put off its dinner—that's us, by the way—by a herd of angry ankylosaurs . . .'

# *Gurrr!*

The albie growled, turning its great head from side to side as the big ankies moved in like a circle of armoured tanks.

'This time, the ankies are determined to see off their deadly enemy,' Tom continued. 'An

 179

albertosaurus is no match for an army that sticks together . . . '

# Thwack!

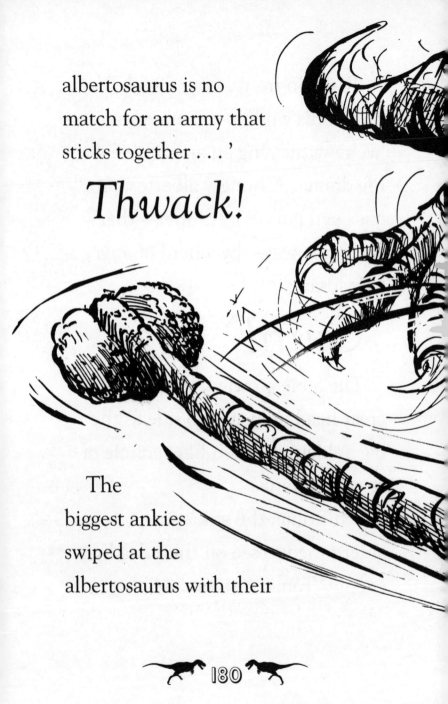

The biggest ankies swiped at the albertosaurus with their

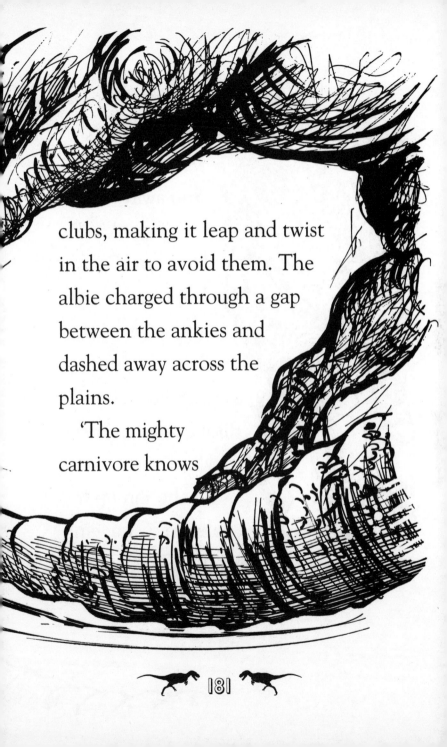

clubs, making it leap and twist
in the air to avoid them. The
albie charged through a gap
between the ankies and
dashed away across the
plains.

'The mighty
carnivore knows

it's outnumbered,'
Tom announced.
'All it can do is
run away . . .'

'Go, ankies!'
Jamie and Tom
leapt in the air
and gave each
other a high five
as the vicious lizard
disappeared over the
skyline.

Nacho ran up to
a baby anky, wagging
his tail as if he wanted
to make friends.

'Nacho, come back!' Jamie yelled as a big anky advanced towards him.

*Swish.*

The anky's tail narrowly missed flattening the puppy.

Nacho's ears dropped and he squatted on the ground as the little anky skittered off with its mother.

'That scared him so much, he's done a poo!' Jamie chuckled.

'You'll have to pick it up,' Tom giggled. 'We can't leave anything here in case it gets fossilized—and that includes puppy poo.'

Jamie sighed and rummaged in his backpack for one of the plastic poo bags Agnes had given him. Wanna and Nacho watched with interest as Jamie reluctantly picked up the steaming pile. It felt warm and squidgy through the bag.

'Ugh!' he muttered, tying a knot in the top of the stinky bag. He wrapped a second bag around the first and gingerly held it by the loop at the top.

'Let's get out of here!' He grabbed Nacho's lead. Tom picked up Wanna's.

Nacho and Wanna sprinted to the river, Tom and Jamie clinging to the leads as the puppy and dino pulled them along. The sandstorm had dumped great piles of sand into the water, making it easy to cross.

Nacho and Wanna
dragged the boys up
Gingko Hill, and they
slithered through the
gingko sludge to the
cave. Jamie stood
beside the trail of
dinosaur footprints
that seemed to lead
magically out of the
rock-face.

'We got back in
double-quick time,'
he panted.

Tom nodded.

'Nacho and Wanna

would make a good team of huskies.'
He untied Wanna's collar and lead.

'It was fun pretending you were a pet, Wanna,' he said. 'But now you have to go back to the wild—until we meet up next time.'

Wanna wagged his tail and picked up a fallen gingko fruit. But instead of gulping it down, he nudged it towards Nacho.

'Awww,' Jamie said, 'he knows it's time to say goodbye.'

Nacho scrunched up his muzzle and took a lick at the stinky fruit.

N . . . n . . . *nacho!* He sneezed.

Then he wagged his tail and nudged
the fruit back to Wanna. The little
dino carefully picked up the gingko
and carried it over to his nest of
twigs in the corner of Gingko Cave.
He gave a deep, contented sigh and
curled up in his bed. Nacho trotted
over and snuggled up next to him.
In an instant, he was fast asleep.
Puppy snores rumbled round the
cave on Gingko Hill.

'He's having his afternoon nap at last,' Tom said, removing Nacho's lead and hoisting the exhausted ball of fluff out of Wanna's bed. Wanna looked up, twitched his tail, and closed his eyes.

'Bye, Wanna,' Tom and Jamie whispered.

Then, with Tom carrying the sleeping Nacho and Jamie holding on tight to the bag of poo, they stepped backwards in Wanna's fresh footprints, and flashed back to their secret cave in Dinosaur Cove.

# CHAPTER 12

Jamie flicked on his torch and shone the light on the poo bag.

'Hope it's turned to dust,' he murmured. But no such luck—it was still fresh and squishy.

Jamie turned the beam of light on Tom and Nacho opened his eyes.

*Woof!*

He squirmed in Tom's arms, jumped to the floor, and trotted to the gap in the secret cave.

'Not again,' groaned Jamie.

'Follow him!' Tom yelled, squeezing through the gap. He chased Nacho through Smugglers' Cave and out into the sunlight on Smuggler's Point.

The puppy picked his way through the boulders and bounded down the path towards the old lighthouse where the Dinosaur

Museum was and Jamie, his dad, and
Grandad lived.

A woman with a floppy hat was
coming up the path.

'Nacho!' Agnes
exclaimed in delight as the
puppy hurled itself into her
arms and licked her face.

'I was looking for you. Where
have you been?'

'He was playing in the caves,'
Tom told Agnes. 'We
were just on our way
back with him.'

'He's had a bit
of an adventure,'
Jamie added.

Tom glanced at Jamie and raised his eyebrows. Agnes had no idea what sort of adventure!

'No wonder he's tired out now,' Agnes said. She stroked Nacho's silky ears. 'I'll take him home for his nap.'

She spotted the poo bag swinging from Jamie's hand.

'Good to see you cleared up after him,' said Agnes, taking the bag. 'I'll put that in the bin on my way home.'

Agnes set off
down the path,
Nacho wriggling in
her arms. He put his
head over Agnes's
shoulder.

*Woof!*

Nacho barked.

*Woof woof!*

'Bye, Nacho,' Tom and Jamie called.

Jamie looked at Tom. 'Dinosaurs are much less trouble than dogs,' he whispered. 'We never have to pick up dino poo!'

'We'd need to take some really big bags with us if we did!' Tom grinned.

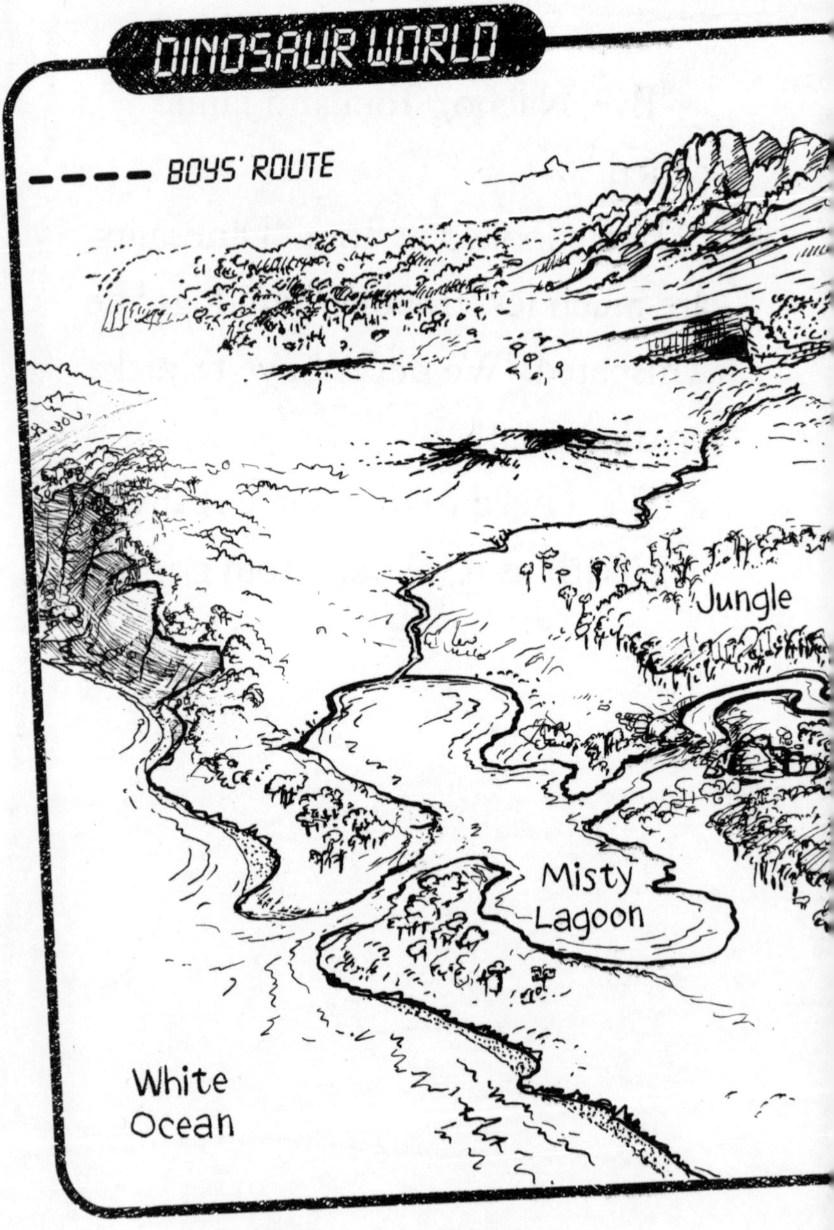

DINOSAUR WORLD

- - - - BOYS' ROUTE

Jungle

Misty Lagoon

White Ocean

198

Far Away Mountains

Crashing
Rock
Falls

Great
Plains

Fang
Rock

Gingko
Hill

# GLOSSARY

**Alamosaurus** (al-am-oh-sor-us) – a gigantic dinosaur with a vegetarian diet that searched for food with its long neck and tiny head while protecting itself with its long, whip-like tail.

**Albertosaurus** (albie) (al-bert-oh-sor-us) – a meat-eating dinosaur with a huge tail and two strong legs, but two tiny arms. It was very similar to tyrannosaurus rex, but smaller.

**Ankylosaurus** (ankie) (an-ki-low-sor-us) – a vegetarian dinosaur known for its armoured coat and clubbed tail. Its armour consisted of large bony bumps similar to the covering of modern-day crocodiles and lizards.

**Corythosaurus** (kor-ith-oh-sor-us) – a duck-billed dinosaur that used hundreds of tiny teeth at the back of its beak to crush and grind plants. It had a rounded bony crest at the back of its head.

**Cretaceous** (cret-ay-shus) – from about 65 to 150 million years ago, this time period was home to the widest variety of dinosaur and insect life of any period. Birds replaced winged dinosaurs, while in the sea, sharks and rays multiplied.

**Gingko** (gink-oh) – a tree native to China called a 'living fossil' because fossils of it have been found dating back millions of years, yet they are still around today. Also known as the stink bomb tree because of its smelly apricot-like fruit.

**Hadrosaurus** (had-ro-sor-us) – a type of plant-eating dinosaur. This family includes the corythosaurus and lambeosaurus. The fronts of these dinosaurs' heads were flat with duck bills, and they had thousands of teeth in the back of their mouths.

**Lambeosaurus** (lam-bee-oh-sor-us) – a vegetarian dinosaur with an axe-shaped crest at the back of its head. It had a small beak and a long straight tail.

**Old English sheepdog** – a large dog with a long, thick, shaggy grey and white coat. It used to be called 'the shepherd's dog' and likes to herd other animals—sometimes even people.

**Pterodactyl** (ter-oh-dak-til) – a flying prehistoric reptile which could be as small as a bird or as large as an aeroplane.

**Sand storm** – a storm caused by loose sand and dust being blown around by strong winds. It looks like a giant, solid wall of moving sand.

**Triceratops** (t-tops) (try-serra-tops) – a three-horned, plant-eating dinosaur which looks like a rhinoceros.

**Utahraptor** (yoo-tah-rap-tor) – a large meat-eating dinosaur. It was a feathered two-legged dinosaur as tall as a giraffe, and had a snout lined with pointy fangs. It is the largest raptor yet discovered. Named after the place it was discovered: Utah in the USA.

**Wannanosaurus** (wah-nan-oh-sor-us) – a dinosaur that only ate plants and used its hard, flat skull to defend itself. Named after the place it was discovered: Wannano in China.

Join Jamie and Tom
in Dino World
with the

# Dinosaur Cove™

## CRETACEOUS SURVIVAL GUIDE

Turn the page for a taster
of all the awesome
things to do . . .

# Create!

## MAKE YOUR OWN EDIBLE DINO POO!

### YOU WILL NEED:

- 100g plain chocolate
- 50g margarine
- 2 tablespoons golden syrup
- 150g plain digestive biscuits

Don't forget to ask a grown-up to help melt the chocolate!

**1** Put the biscuits in a large freezer bag and tie the bag shut. Using a rolling pin, bash the biscuits into crumbs.

**2** Break up the chocolate into pieces and put them in a saucepan. Heat the pan on a low temperature until the chocolate has melted.

**3** Stir the margarine and syrup into the melted chocolate.

**4** Take the saucepan off the heat. Pour the biscuit crumbs into the chocolate mixture and stir together.

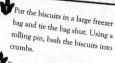

# Play!

## WHICH CRETACEOUS DINO ARE YOU?

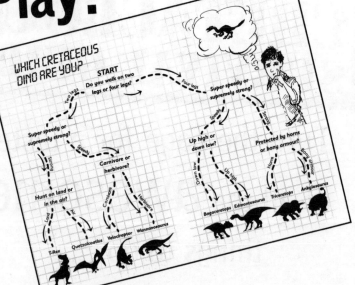

START
Do you walk on two legs or four legs?

Two legs — Super speedy or supremely strong?
Speedy — Carnivore or herbivore?
Carnivore — Hunt on land or in the air?
Land — T-Rex
Air — Quetzalcoatlus
Herbivore — Velociraptor
Wannanosaurus

Four legs — Super speedy or supremely strong?
Speedy — Up high or down low?
Down low — Bagaceratops
Up high — Edmontosaurus
Strong — Protected by horns or bony armour?
Horns — Triceratops
Bony armour — Ankylosaurus

# Discover!

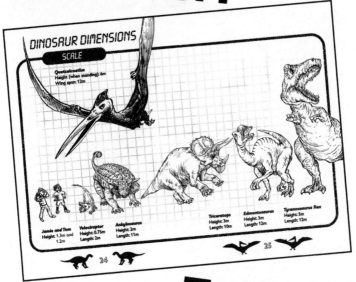

DINOSAUR DIMENSIONS
SCALE

Quetzalcoatlus
Height (when standing): 6m
Wing span: 12m

Jamie and Tom
Height: 1.3m and 1.2m

Velociraptor
Height: 0.75m
Length: 2m

Ankylosaurus
Height: 2m
Length: 11m

Triceratops
Height: 3m
Length: 10m

Edmontosaurus
Height: 3m
Length: 12m

Tyrannosaurus Rex
Height: 5m
Length: 12m

24    25

# Explore!

### T-REX: THE LIZARD KING

Tyrannosaurus Rex was a carnivore that ate all sorts of other creatures, from small dinosaurs like velociraptors to large ones like edmontosaurs. Palaeontologists think the t-rex was probably a scavenger as well as a hunter, eating up the remains of creatures that had already died. With chisel-shaped teeth at the front and huge teeth with knife-like serrated edges filling the rest of its mouth, the t-rex was a fearsome predator. The biggest t-rex skull ever found is 150cm long and was discovered in the 1960s. The biggest and best preserved whole t-rex skeleton is in the Field Museum of Natural History in Chicago. Its name is FMNH PR 2081, but its nickname is Sue.